IGNORE THE TROLLS

WRITTEN BY
JORDAN GERSHOWITZ

ILLUSTRATED BY
SANDHYA PRABHAT

POW! BROOKLYN

GOOD MORROW

and welcome
to the majestic kingdom of Holly Hills.
From the merry mermaids, to the sincere centaurs,
to the energetic elves, Holly Hills is a place
filled with the most wonderful, magical creatures.

But it's not all rainbows and unicorns.
For you see, Holly Hills has a dreaded curse.
This land is overrun by evil, nasty trolls!

The realm is also home to
Tim The Timid,
a boy who is too shy
to dance with fairies,

too nervous
to play with giants,
and too scared
to pet fire-breathing dragons.

While Tim may be meek, he has a great big heart.
He shares his lunch with hungry gnomes,

he helps yetis
with their
homework,

and he always
jokes around with
the lonely cyclops.

Tim longs to cast his timidity aside.

Ye Olde
School Bus

Every day, he rides
the bus and dreams of
being a part of the bravest
group at school, the Knights!

For the Knights are without fear
and display their valor on the jousting field. Loved by all, a Knight
would never be afraid of fairies, or giants, or fire-breathing dragons.

"Maybe if I join the Knights,"
Tim thinks,
"I'll become courageous,
just like them.

Instead of Tim the Timid,
I'll be known as

TIM THE TERRIFIC

Then one day, Tim gets his opportunity.
Not by a witch's spell, but by his teacher's decree.

In 3 Days' Time
TRYOUTS
Will Be Held
For The
JOUSTING TEAM

NAMES

"This is my chance!" he tells himself.
"I can finally show everyone
why I should be a Knight."

However, fear and self-doubt soon take over.
"What if I'm not good enough?
What if everyone makes fun of me?
What if I embarrass myself so bad I have to
fly off on a griffin, never to return?"

Tim the Timid lives up to his name.
He slinks back, too frightened to sign up.

Amongst the crowd, Tim spots a friendly face.
It's a Knight named
Bethany The Brave.

"Tim, you must try out!!" Bethany declares.
"The most important part of being a Knight is having a big heart.
And I know no one who has a bigger heart than you."

Tim smiles. This is just what he needed to hear.
Encouraged, he grabs a pen and writes down his name.
He shall try out after all.

"But there is one thing you should know," Bethany warns.
"Whatever you do, you must ignore the trolls."

NAMES

James
IGOR
Viktoria

Now in his courtyard,
Tim is ready to prove himself.
He grabs a lance and tries
to knock over his target.

It doesn't go well.

Behind him,
Tim hears an evil laugh.
He turns to see a nasty troll
waving a magic picture taker.

The troll cackles,
"You're a loser,
Tim the Timid.
You'll never be
good enough
to be a Knight!"

timid

Tim is wounded by these words.
This was his greatest fear.
Maybe the troll is right.
Maybe he isn't good enough.

Tim knows
Bethany the Brave
told him to ignore the trolls,
but he can't help himself.
He must show this brute
he can be courageous.

"I will be a Knight!"
Tim cries out.
"Just wait and see!"

The troll laughs even harder,
which only makes Tim feel worse.

The next morning,
Tim sees two kids snicker
as they pass a scroll
to one another.

It's the embarrassing
picture of him.
This must be the work
of that troll!

Tim tries to hide his embarrassment
when Bethany the Brave sits next to him.
She saw the scroll too.

Tim sighs, "I wish a wizard
could make that picture disappear."

"You're getting troll'd,"

Bethany says as she pats her friend on the back.
"But don't worry,
as long as you ignore the trolls,
you'll be a Knight soon enough!"

Alas,

Tim still doesn't listen to his friend.

After school,
a determined Tim
finds the troll and proclaims,
"Hear me now.
I am good enough to be a Knight
and I shall prove it!"

But as Tim shows off his skills, he trips over his feet and falls.
Just then, a second troll appears, its lips curled in a sneer.

The two monsters gang up and shout out,
"Give up, Tim!
You stink worse than an ogre
after a mud bath!"

Persistent,
Tim grits his teeth and tries again.
But it's still no use.
He fails over and over and over,
with each disastrous attempt
bringing more and more trolls.

The vile villains chuckle at Tim's misfortune
and take photos with their magic picture takers.
They tease him with their unkind words
and share the news across the land,
"Hear ye! Hear ye!
Tim isn't a real Knight
and he never will be!"

"Stop it!"
Tim cries out.
"That's not true!"

The more Tim battles,
the more the trolls multiply.
Soon, Tim's courtyard is overrun!
Surrounded, Tim throws down his lance
and runs away in tears.

The next day,
Tim finds a flock of blue birds
tweeting the news
in the cafeteria.

Students share
embarrassing scrolls
of Tim in class.

Even when Tim signs onto his orb,
he can't escape the torment.
No matter where he goes, word follows.
It seems as if the entire school
is swarming with trolls.

Tim the Timid hangs his head.
He wishes he had
an invisibility potion
so he could just vanish.

"I give up,"
a defeated Tim tells Bethany.
"I can't be a Knight,
I'm just a shy, timid boy.
That's what I was born to be."

"You can't give up!
You were getting better!"

"I wasn't," Tim sniffles.
"All of the trolls said so."

Bethany perks up.
"The trolls?!
What did I tell you?"

"You told me
to ignore them."

"And did you?"

Tim shakes his head no.
Bethany puts her arm around her friend.
"In order to stop the trolls," she says,
"you have to understand what they are..."

"Trolls are mean creatures who enjoy making people upset by tearing them down, especially those who take risks and try something new.

But the one thing you can't do is let them get under your skin."

"They can get under your skin?!" Tim screams.

"No, silly. I mean, you can't let them bother you," Bethany reassures. "You know who you really are, and that's most important. Just because the trolls say something, doesn't make it true."

"How do you know so much
about trolls?" Tim asks.

Bethany pulls out a scroll from her bag.
"I wasn't always brave.
Before I joined the Knights,
I was known as Bethany the Bashful.
I was like you. I also got troll'd."

BETHANY the BASHFUL

"Unfortunately, there's no magic spell
to be rid of trolls forever.
But you can make them disappear,"
Bethany says proudly.

"Tell me!" Tim desperately exclaims.
"I must know how to vanquish
them before the tryouts tomorrow!"

Bethany smiles and tells Tim
if he wants the trolls to disappear,
all he has to do is **ignore them**.

Tim smiles and grabs his lance.
He will listen to Bethany.
He will finally ignore the trolls!

The next morning, Tim is nervous.
He's nervous as he rides the bus,
he's nervous as he sits through class,
and he's nervous when the final bell rings.

Ye Final
~Bell~

It's time for
the tryouts!

On the field,
Tim struggles to mount his horse.
The trolls start to laugh.

"Here we go again..."

IGNORE THEM

YOU CAN DO IT!

But this time
is different.
Tim doesn't listen to them.
"Just ignore the trolls,"
he tells himself.

The trolls' laughter
bounces off of Tim, as if he were wearing enchanted armor.

Feeling their powers weaken,
the trolls shout out mean names and make funny faces.
But Tim doesn't pay attention. He holds his head high and rides.

Suddenly, something magical happens.
One by one, the trolls starts to vanish, until there is only a single troll left.
The one who started it all.

But it too is no match for Tim's spirit.
No mean names or tweeting birds or embarrassing pictures
can stop Tim now.

Tim wields his lance and knocks down his target.
HUZZAH!

"I knew you could do it!" Bethany the Brave beams as she hands Tim his new jacket. "Everyone, it is my great honor to welcome our newest Knight, Tim the Terrific!"

The gnomes, the yetis, and the cyclops all erupt in applause.
As do the fairies Tim was too shy to dance with, the giants he was too nervous
to play with, and the fire-breathing dragons he was too afraid to pet.
The entire realm now knows how courageous Tim really is.

Tim's dream may have come true, but he knows his quest is not over.
While he overcame the trolls, others will not.
As a true Knight, it's Tim's duty to help those in need.

"From this day forth," Tim swears, "it will be
my greatest honor to protect those who are afflicted.
We must spread the word, far and wide.
If we ignore the trolls, they will be powerless!"

So whether you live in the magical kingdom
of Holly Hills or some other far-away land,
just remember the tale of Tim.

For you have it in you to be terrific,
no matter what the trolls say.

For anyone who's
ever been troll'd.
-J.G.

To my parents
–champion troll-ignorers.
-S.P.

Ignore the Trolls

Text © 2019 by Jordan Gershowitz
Illustrations © 2019 by Sandhya Prabhat

Published by POW! a division of
powerHouse Packaging & Supply, Inc.
32 Adams Street,
Brooklyn, NY 11201-1021

info@POWkidsBooks.com

Printed by Asia Pacific Offset

Book design by Krzysztof Poluchowicz

Library of Congress Control Number: 2019941651

ISBN: 978-1-57687-933-7

10 9 8 7 6 5 4 3 2 1

Printed and bound in China